To my friend Alessandra

Text and illustrations copyright © 2007 by Mo Willems

For information address Hyperion Books for Children,
114 Fifth Avenue, New York, New York 10011-5690.
Printed in Singapore
Reinforced binding

First Edition
10 9 8 7 6 5 4 3
F850-6835-5-10159

Library of Congress Cataloging-in-Publication Data
Today I will fly!/by Mo Willems.—1st ed.
p. cm.— (An Elephant and Piggie book)
Summary: While Piggie is determined to fly, Elephant is skeptical, but when Piggie gets
a little help from others, amazing things happen.
ISBN-10: 1-4231-0295-9 (alk. paper)
ISBN-13: 978-1-4231-0295-3
[1. Pigs—Fiction. 2. Elephants—Fiction. 3. Cooperativeness—Fiction.
4. Friendship—Fiction.] I. Title.
PZ7.W65535To 2007
[Fic]—dc22
2006049621

Visit www.hyperionbooksforchildren.com and www.pigeonpresents.com

Today I Will Fly!

By **Mo Willems**

An **ELEPHANT & PIGGIE** Book

Hyperion Books for Children/*New York*

Today I will fly!

4

You will not fly today.

You will not fly tomorrow.

You will not fly
next week.

Good-bye.

She will not fly.

Fly, fly, fly, fly, fly,

fly, fly, fly, fly, fly!

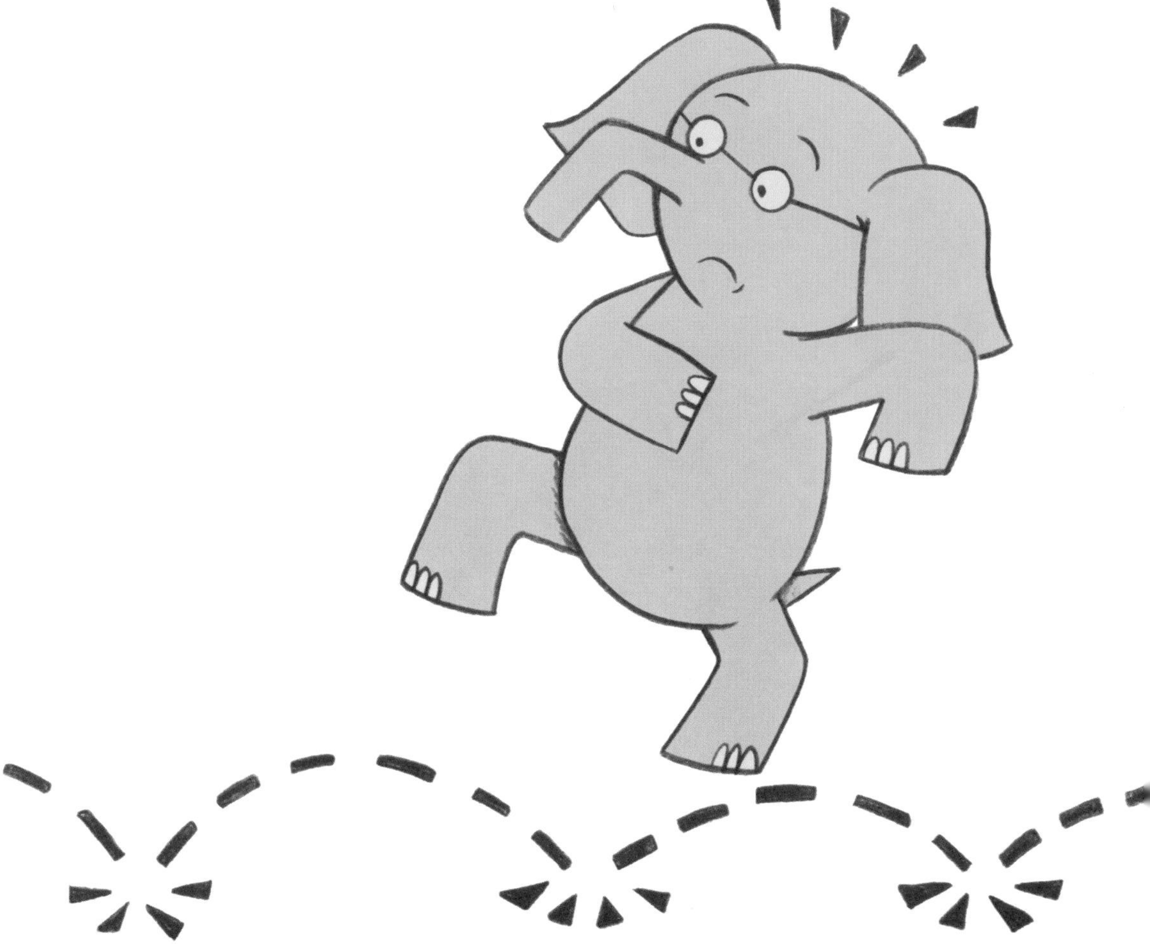

Fly, fly, fly, fly!

You need help.

I will get help!

19

23

It was a big jump!

Yes, it was a big jump.
But you did not fly.

I will eat lunch.

Good-bye!

Fly! Fly! Fly!

I do need help.

I will.
I will help you.

Thank you.

Hello?

Hello!

You are flying today!

I am *not* flying!

I am getting help.

Tomorrow *I* will fly!

Good luck.